CW00848302

First published in 1996 by Sapling,
an imprint of Boxtree Ltd, Broadwall House,
21 Broadwall, London SE1 9PL
Copyright © Geoffrey Planer, 1996

10 9 8 7 6 5 4 3 2 1

Reproduction by SX Composing DTP
Printed and bound in Great Britain by Cambus Litho Ltd.

ISBN: 0 7522 2315 1

A CIP catalogue entry for this book
is available from the British Library.

MOUSE TALES

Mr and Mrs Cat

Geoffrey Planer

sapling

For a very special Jan
(who started it all)

'Daddy?'

'Yes,' said Mr Tail.

'Why do we have
mummies and daddies?'

'What?' said Mr Tail,
raising an eyebrow.

'Why?' asked Vanessa.

'Er, it's a long story.'

'Good. Can I have it, then?
You promised.'

'Promised what?'

'A long story,' said Vanessa.

'I don't remember that,' said Mr Tail.

'You said if I was good.'

'Well, were you?'

'A bit.'

'A bit of a story it is, then,'
he said, and he took her
upstairs on his back.

Another Night,
Another Mouse,
Another Tale . . .

Mr and Mrs Cat

There was once a Mr Cat who lived in a house with his four kittens. They didn't have a Mrs Cat because, very sadly, she had died some years before. But they were quite happy.

Now, there is an
awful lot for a
Mr Cat to do
each day, looking
after four kittens
and a house.

There are
breakfasts and
beds to make,
teeth and
clothes to wash,
socks and
toys to mend,
dishes and
noses to scrub,
chimneys and
floors to sweep.

Mr Cat also had to go out each day to get some money. He had so much to do each day, and was terribly, terribly busy in the morning and terribly, terribly busy in the evening

and terribly, terribly busy at the weekend,
doing all the other sorts of jobs that
needed doing after his work.

The trouble was that while Mr Cat
was terribly, terribly good at his
proper job (sometimes),

he was terribly, terribly bad at doing the
other jobs. It was always rush, rush, rush.

He would put
tea on the toast

and jam in
the juice.

He'd pour milk
in the pasta
and butter
the books.

He'd wash faces with floorcloths and dishes with dusters. He'd clean cookers with chocolate and carpets with custard.

Once he covered the telephone
with chocolate spread.

Once he put soap in the soup.

He would also ...

put socks
on tails,

knickers
on heads,

dresses on
backwards
... and ...

leave kittens
in cupboards.

And he'd leave
cups in beds.

And he'd leave
dishes on
doormats.

And he'd drop
doughnuts
down drains.

And sometimes he'd
even forget to put
on his own shoes.

Mr Cat would bake bagels and broccoli or fry ice-cream and fruit salad. Mr Cat might cook chocolate and cheese puffs or boil baked beans and blueberries. Mr Cat once roasted rice and rum-babas and grilled carrots and cream.

So, although Mr Cat and the four kittens
were happy, one had to say that they
and the kitchen and the house
were all a dreadful mess.

Now, in the house opposite lived
a Mrs Cat (whose husband had also
sadly died some years before)
with her one kitten.

Their house was always spotless.
Mrs Cat cleaned it upstairs and
downstairs before breakfast.

Her kitten was also
spotless. She cleaned
her upstairs and
downstairs before
breakfast, too.

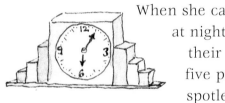

When she came home
at night, they ate
their supper at
five past six off
spotless plates,

and they both
went to their
spotless beds
at eight twenty-
six each night.

Mr Cat's four kittens would look out of
their window longingly as Mrs Cat and
her kitten ate their scrumptious suppers.

Now, one evening, just as usual,
Mr Cat arrived home late. The kittens
were waiting for their supper, but when
he looked in the fridge all he found
was a hammer and a hat and a
dolly with no clothes on.

No food. The
shops were
all shut.
What to do?
What to do?

The younger
kittens started
crying.

The older kittens
brought the
phone over
to Mr Cat.

Mr Cat summoned up his courage and
spoke to Mrs Cat to ask if she might,
very kindly and if it would not be any
trouble, lend him a small loaf of bread
and enough butter for five slices. Mrs Cat
came over with a loaf straight away and
looked at Mr Cat (and the mess) in
an old fashioned sort of way.

In no time at all she had washed floors,
wiped walls, brushed whiskers, cleaned
pots, curled tails and cooked a delicious
herringbone soufflé (the best the
four kittens had ever tasted).

Mr Cat looked across the room at
Mrs Cat in an old fashioned sort of way.
Now Mrs Cat did not let Mr Cat have it
easy just because he couldn't look after
his family. Oh no. He had to bring her
flowers and write her old fashioned love
letters. Oh yes, she took her time.

But in the end they did get married
and they all moved into one big house
together and lived there pretty
happily for a very long time.

(Only the kittens didn't like having
their faces washed every morning)

'I don't think that's a true story,' said Vanessa.
'Absolutely,' said Mr Tail as he tucked her up.
'How do you know?'
'I know Mr Cat personally,' said Mr Tail.
'A cat?' said Vanessa. 'I don't believe you.'
'Some cats can be most personable,' said Mr Tail.
'You're fibbing,' said Vanessa.
'Tall tales, small tales ... sleepy time for all Tails,'
said Mr Tail as he kissed Vanessa good night.
And then he tiptoed round the house and kissed
the 364 other little Tails good night too.

Small Tales,
Tall Tales,
Bedtime -
for All Tails